The Mask

MILA CRAWFORD

Author Notes

Dear Reader,

This novella contains content that could be disturbing to some readers, please read at your own risk.

-Somnoph!l!@, Degrad@tion, Prim@l Play, Praise, Sp!t pl@y, Breath Play, CNC, Dubcon. Fear play

-Play with sharp objects used to cut up fruits, and vegetables.

-Play with things that go Pew Pew

-Violence and violent acts

-Parental loss

Also by Mila Crawford

These are all stand alones within the same wold.

Bound Together

Room Twenty-Two

Thicker Than Blood

Hide snd Seek

The Mask

Stay Connected

Website

Amazon

TikTok

Facebook

Instagram

GoodReads

Prologue

Mikhail

Mom's not screaming. She was a few moments ago. Now she's making gasping sounds and keeps coughing and swallowing. It's the same sound my dad made while mom cried and shrieked, so she must be dying.

I always thought people would yell into the void and argue with anyone who would listen when they drew. But it seems the last moments of life are like a terrible bout of pneumonia or bronchitis.

The smell of microwave popcorn still lingers in the air, mixed with something I've never smelled before. Maybe it's fear or the urine now soaking my pants.

We were watching a movie on the couch when the bad people showed up at our small apartment. Mom put out a spread of all my favorites. Dad jumped up and went to the "Mik can't touch" box and unlocked it. He pulled out a gun. I didn't even know we owned one or that my father knew how to use it. But the way his hand worked it, he looked like one of the G.I. Joe cartoons I watch.

Mom tugged at my shirt. I told her I wanted to watch the movie, but she pulled until I had to go with her. I gazed longingly at the popcorn sitting on the chipped wooden coffee table.

She rushed me into the closet, piled every piece of clothing she could find on top of me and told me to be quiet.

So I'm here, silent and buried under a mountain of coats, scarves, and sweaters. All I want to do is yell, cry, or both, but Mom begged me not to make a sound, so I won't. She was sad when she looked at me, and I didn't want to make her sad. I like it when she's smiling and happy.

It's so dark here. I don't like the dark. Mom usually lets me have a light on at night to keep the monsters away. But the monsters are here, in our apartment. I hear them breaking things. Yelling at each other with booming voices. They talk so loudly as if they don't care about the neighbors. Mom says it's rude not to care about other people. These men obviously don't have a wonderful mom like mine. Someone to teach them good manners.

The skin around my eyes is tight as if it's being stretched on all sides. Mom said if I closed my eyes with all my might, the monsters wouldn't be able to find me. So I focus on the darkness and hope it's not like the lies of Santa Claus she told me when I was younger.

Loud footsteps stop. I don't dare peek to see if they're on the other side of the small encasing of the closet. I focus on the darkness. It's not as frightening as before because my fear of the dark is in my mind, whereas the fear of the men is in my soul. Fearing things in your imagination differs from fearing things in your reality. There is no night light to protect me now.

"They've got a kid."

A shiver of dread runs down my spine at the icy-crisp voice. Mom warned me about men like them. She

3

called them Devils and said we have to watch for them before they come to take our souls.

"Yes, a little boy. I think the file said he was nine."

Ten. I'm ten. I had a birthday last week. Mom and Dad got me a cake, a new sweater, and dinner at McDonald's. I wanted an Xbox like Billy Montgomery down the hall, but money was tight, and my parents couldn't swing it.

"He has to be here. They have no friends, no family. The kid wouldn't be in school, and they have no money for extracurriculars. Look at this place. It's a fuckin' dump."

It's not a dump. It's our home. A small voice in my mind tells me to be quiet, that it doesn't matter what this guy says.

"Check under the beds, closets, under fuckin' cupboards. Pull every floorboard for all I care. Fuck, burn the entire building to get this kid out if you have to."

Burn the building? What about Billy and his little sister? They can't burn the building. Mrs. Rogers down the hall is ninety. She won't be able to run for her life. If they burn the building, they'll kill me, but they'll kill everyone else, too.

I push the clothes off me and get up as the closet door flies open, and a giant man with a long, jagged scar on his face looms over me. But it's not his scar I focus on. It's the hollow, moss green of his eyes.

The man barks a snide laugh before his hand curls around my shirt collar and he yanks me outside, where I see the blood-soaked carpet and my parents' lifeless bodies on the floor.

"Can I close my eyes when you kill me?" I ask, my voice as dead as the man's eyes.

"Kill you? Nah, we're not gonna kill you."

I squint, too frightened to stare at the man directly. "What are you going to do with me?"

"I don't know what Sergei Fedorov wants to do with you." He nods toward my mother's body. "We were told to kill anyone who got in our way. But for your sake, kid, I hope that man kills you cause he's not known for being kind."

My fear is so consuming that I swear my bones shake with it. What's worse than death, and do I want to find out?

They drape a black hood over my eyes, shrouding me in darkness. But this time, the darkness isn't shutting out the monsters—it's welcoming them.

"Let's get out of here. Grab the kid," the other man orders, and once again, my collar is gripped so tightly that it cuts into my throat.

We travel for what feels like hours or a day. I'm not sure. They've locked me up in a crate like a dog. I want to cry, but Dad always said not to show them tears. He said that's when they know they've got you. I'm scared I'll piss my pants again. Then my tears won't matter as much. One of them already made a point about how gross I smell. I push my shoulders back. Dad said always meet your death like a man. Men don't pee their pants. But then again, I'm not a man. I'm a scared boy.

Harsh, blaring sunlight stings my eyes as I try to focus on the face above me. It's not the hollow-eyed man. This is someone new. His face is pudgier, and a cigar burns in his large hand. He has a smile on his face, and it's not a scary one. He looks kind, but that's probably a mirage because he's connected to the two who just murdered my parents. And murderers aren't good people.

"You hungry?"

He has a thick Russian accent like my dad. That's stupidly comforting to me. Familiar. I don't respond, but my stomach growls, betraying me.

He reaches his hand out to me. "Come on, then."

I take it, but I don't want to. It's a reflex because I'm frightened of what will happen if I don't.

'What's your name?" he asks kindly.

"Mikhail Smirnov."

I gaze around the room. A kitchen—if you can call it that. The space is larger than our two-bedroom apartment in Chicago. The floors look like glass, beige with flecks of black and white in them. They're kind of cool looking. I've only ever seen floors like this in movies. Rich people have floors like this.

"My name is Sergei." He leads me to a black island in the middle of the room and gestures for me to take a seat. Once I'm seated, he sits directly across from me. "You like burgers, Mikhail?"

I nod. My throat is so dry I'm not sure I can say anymore.

"How rude of me," Sergei says, pushing a glass of water toward me. "Mikhail, would you like to live here? It's a big house, and I have two little boys. Maxim and Alexie. One's your age and another a few years younger."

Live here? What the heck is this guy thinking? He's just killed my parents and now wants me to live with him? Is he a pedophile? Nothing about this is normal. Then again, having your parents brutally murdered in your apartment isn't normal either.

"Why did you kill my parents?"

He picks up his glass, half the size of mine, and swirls the liquid. "I killed your mother."

"I saw the bodies. Both my mother and father were lying dead on the ground."

"Once again, I didn't kill your parents. I only killed your mother."

"Why?"

"Because she took something that belongs to me. The only way to get it back was to get rid of her."

"What did she take?"

"You."

Chapter One

M ikhail

Hunt Club—a large house in the Forest Glen neighborhood in Chicago—makes the depraved fantasies of the rich a reality.

Unlike other sex clubs, it only caters to one kink. Primal. And this isn't the primal people read in romance novels where the girl frolics in the forest until the man catches her and then makes passionate love to her. Kinky, but in a sweet, safe way that's palatable to the masses.

This place feeds monsters and encourages debauchery. It's where animals come to stalk their prey and rip them apart limb by limb until they satiate the monster within.

They nestled the house in the middle of lush forests and ten acres of land. Some rich Chicago financier owns the place, Loren Miller. I did a background check on him. Grandfather was close with Al Capone. Family has old money, but it's tainted with controversy, and his brother is serving a sentence in upstate New York for killing his wife, which he adamantly denies. But even with all the controversy surrounding them, you wouldn't know it as you gaze upon the who's who of Chicago's upper crust. The Miller money and affluence have protected them well, at least on a superficial level.

I scan the large living room, the ostentatious chandeliers dangling from cream vaulted ceilings, void spaces with off-white leather furniture strategically placed in dark corners, and the crisp white rugs adorning the gold-fleck-covered marble floors.

The hard liquor coats my throat as I drown my vodka on the rocks, slamming the glass on the bar. Yes, the house has a legit bar in the middle of it. An oddity in most houses, it's more fitting for a dance club in Soho.

"This won't cut it," I declare.

"Do you ever relax?" my buddy Axel asks as his hand mindlessly rubs his girl's back. "Stella and I do this all the time. I'm telling you, you'll get what you need."

I glower at him. "How the fuck do you control someone else chasing Stella?"

Axel shrugs, beaming at Stella. "It's never happened. But I suppose the animal in me might have to snap a neck."

My eyes roam the room. Men and women talk casually like they aren't about to indulge in sexual mayhem. Shooting the shit about mundane things like the weather and movies they like as if it's normal when everyone's here to fuck like animals.

"So, you gonna take the mask off?" Axel asks, his eyes roaming my face.

Out of habit, I raise my hand to my face, and my fingertips brush against the white plastic mask I've worn for over twenty years. The only time I take it off is when I sleep. No one alive has seen what I look like, not even my best friends. "Nope. Unless I want to turn this sex orgy into a bloodbath."

"You can't be serious about killing someone just for seeing your face?"

Axel is a good guy, but the hypocrisy dripping off his tongue is enough to make me want to slam his head against the bar and revel in the blood oozing out. "You kill men for looking at Stella, but I can't if someone sees my face?"

"Stella is my life. I consider that self-defense."

A burst of laughter escapes my lips. It's so loud that various pairs of eyes in the room glare at me. Usually, I'd bash their heads in for looking at me with such contempt, but this isn't the time to lose my shit and slit some throats. "My mask is important to me. It provides a barrier. It protects me in a way." Truthful words spoken in a rare moment when I show one of my brothers my vulnerability.

"What are you gonna do when you finally meet someone?"

I take a moment to ponder his question, even though I know the answer instantly. I'll never meet someone because you let your guard down when you allow yourself to love. And for various fucked up reasons, my walls never lower. I never want to love someone so much that losing them would bring me to my knees.

Sure, I love my friends—they're family, and I'd take a bullet for them, but losing them wouldn't feel like my heart was being sliced up into a million tiny pieces by the edge of a sharp knife. So I've kept myself hidden, an impenetrable stone mass with a blank face that keeps everyone at bay.

"I meet people all the time. Still kept the mask on."

"Way to go at being obtuse, Mik," Stella says, smiling slyly at me.

"Stella, my love, I'll never meet a good woman because the best one on the planet is taken." I wag my eyebrows when Axel growls and glares at me, nostrils flaring. "Unless you want to add one more to your menagerie?"

"Watch it," Axel warns.

"Relax, buddy. I'm not sure I want you anywhere near my dick."

"You couldn't handle my anaconda."

"I can handle it, pretty boy. I just don't want to."

Stella laughs. "Okay, fellas, we don't need to get to where you both whip it out and start measuring on the bar." She turns her gaze to me. "You sure you want to do this, Mik? It's a little intense."

Intense.

Sweet Stella thinks I'm less fuckin' depraved than the three psychos she's surrounded herself with. She doesn't realize that my need for dominance and blood extends beyond my job and bleeds into how my cock gets hard. The only issue is that most women don't look fondly on you hurting them to get off. And as fucked up as I am, I draw the line at taking someone's will. I'm many fucking things, but I'm not a coward, and forcing a woman to do something against her will is the pathology of a fucking loser.

"You don't have to worry about me, Stella. You need to worry about the poor woman I chase."

Chapter Two

B ree

B reathe in. Breathe out. Repeat.

The ice cubes in my glass ricochet off each other because of the non-stop nervous tremors in my hand. As hard as I try to keep calm, I can't. I keep thinking this is the worst idea I've ever had. There isn't a friendly face in the room. I've thrust myself into the unknown with strangers.

This was a bad idea.

Fetlife—an online social media for kinksters—was one thing, but to come to a weird sex club in the middle of a forest hoping to get what I need without a friendly face in sight? That seems a little idiotic.

I've got a tiny problem. Okay, maybe it's not tiny. I can only come when I'm scared. I've seen a therapist about it and used all kinds of sex toys. Joined Fetlife and explored kinks, and not once have I been able to hit the holy O. The closest I've come is with this guy who shoved a pillow over my face, but then he chickened out and killed the whole mood. I'm twenty- four years old and I've never come. The thing is, what I need to come is something most sane people aren't willing to do.

I need to be petrified.

I need to be submerged in utter fear, like I'm going to die or think I'm going to be mutilated by my sexual partner. Fucked up, right? In the grand scheme, never coming isn't the worst thing to happen to someone. I could've been an exemplary nun if I was a good little Catholic.

I found out immersed in a horror movie marathon. I never got aroused unless I watched one of those. My heart would pump, my brain would start playing tricks on me, my breathing sped up, and my pussy got wet. I mean *wet*. It was the first time I discovered I didn't need lube to make myself wet for penetration.

Deranged, that's what I thought I was. Sick and twisted with no moral compass, no decency— a twisted fuck like the masked men holding sharp objects doused in crimson red.

I rushed to the therapist's office, asking her to commit me, worried I was insane, a danger. She stayed calm, looked at me, and smiled. I didn't know why she was smiling. I mean, it's a little weird for someone to tell you that when they see Ghostface, or Michael chasing someone, they get hot and bothered. She stared me right in the eyes and told me it wasn't as strange as I thought. Explained that fear caused adrenaline release in my body, which got my motor going. She continued to tell me it was like any other kink, and all I needed to do was find someone whose kinks complimented mine.

My friend, Serafina, who I met at Fetlife, told me to try a hunt. A high-paced, no holds barred, animalistic chase leading to sex or, hopefully, some type of release. That's how I found myself here, at The Hunt Club.

"You have your safe word, sweetheart?" a pretty woman with dark black hair, ruby red lips, curves for days, and luminescent skin, asks.

She's wearing a corset and fishnet stockings, and her massive perky breasts are on display as she bends down to pick up a discarded glass off the crystal coffee table.

I quickly fidget with my exposed cleavage, suddenly feeling insecure. "Sorry," I say, shaking my head to clear the fog.

"The safe word. You know it?"

"No. I don't think so."

Her silver tray clangs as she places it on the table in front of me. "First time, huh, honey?"

I nod.

Her smile is sweet and warm. She seems kind. "You don't need to worry. We make sure the prey is safe, no matter what."

"So, what am I missing here?"

"They'll call you for formation. When you hear the bell, you run. Run far, run fast, climb trees, and let the inner doe out. After a certain amount of time, they release the predators. Make sure you pick the right one, honey. Some of these people are animals with no ounce of humanity. The only reason they follow the rules is because they fear those who will hunt them if they don't." She scans the room. "There." She points to a tall man with broad shoulders and a creepy white mask on his face. "Try to get him."

I squeeze my thighs together, trying to avoid the flutter in my vagina. The man might talk directly to my kink, but self-preservation controls my brain. At least at this moment. "Are you crazy? The dude has a mask on his face. He looks like he walked straight out of a Friday the 13th movie."

She pats my thigh like a maternal grandmother, even though she's probably younger than I am, if not the same age. "He might look scary, but he's not a pig. Notice how he's not checking out anyone. He's here with a mission. A man like that won't fuck around. He won't use you like a piece of meat for his pleasure. It's a partner he wants. He'll search for prey who will fight, someone he can respect. It's important to pick a play partner who will respect the rules, and honey, that man may look scary, but he's way better than that guy on the sofa."

I turn to look at a clean-cut blond guy in a classic fit three-piece suit sipping his beer while his hand is groping for the girl beside him.

"That guy doesn't respect women."

"She could be his girlfriend," I suggest.

"Oh, no, honey, that's not his girl."

His hand falls off the girl's ass when a brunette comes closer, abandoning his plaything to kiss the dark-haired girl on the cheek.

"That girl is his woman, honey. Poor thing doesn't know she's with a slimy reptile." She shakes her head and looks at the woman wistfully. "Oh, I got off track, didn't I? Your word is red if you want the play to stop and yellow if you want him to slow down. Remember, honey, use red if it's too much, okay? Some predators take it a little too far."

I nod, smiling at her. Inside, dueling voices scream at me. Questions about how bad this thing becomes that she feels the need to prepare me for it extensively. How dark do some predators get? Then the other voice taunts me with words of encouragement, telling me this is exactly what I need. This is what I want. To be hunted.

"Well, I've got to make the rounds." She rises, picks the tray up, and adjusts it in her hands. "You have fun out there and be safe, honey."

My eyes roam from my now empty cocktail glass to the man with no face. His head is tilted back, shoulders moving up and down. He appears to be laughing at whatever the guy beside him said. I keep staring at him, wondering if the mask is to hide him from the masses. Is he someone important who doesn't want anyone to recognize him, or is the mask about something else?

I'm caught up in my thoughts and ideas about this man when his head shoots up, and he gazes directly at me. His eyes connect with mine. Bright blue, haunted irises, like nothing I've ever seen before. Hypnotic, clear, and feral like a wolf. They captivate me in their trance from across a crowded room.

Chapter Three

Mikhail

So pretty." Stella. She's talking to me, but I can only focus on the little mouse sitting across the room.

In a room over-saturated with half-naked women, she's the only one who's caught my attention, and all she's wearing is a simple dress that falls above her knees. She looks young and sweet, which sticks out like a sore thumb, in a place like this. Her ankles are crossed, and she appears meek, helpless even. The girl is completely out of her element. Her dark eyes are captivating, a rich brown that could easily be

24

mistaken for black like the raven locks falling past her shoulders.

Nothing I've seen in life surpasses her beauty. She's captivating. My cock thinks so, too, since it surged to life the moment she set her almond-shaped eyes on me. She never breaks eye contact, our own secret game of chicken.

Yet something is disturbing her. I don't want to think it's because of me since I make everyone around me uneasy, even those closest to me. Her long delicate fingers fidget with her empty glass, and her knees move subtly from left to right. A girl like her in a place like this should be a little hesitant. This place isn't for the weak of heart, but that she even walked in these doors is enough to gain my respect. She must be taking part in the hunt. Why else would she come here?

A snap of fingers. "Earth to Mik." Stella's voice. She's talking to me, but I'm not sure what she said.

"Yeah?"

"I said she's pretty."

She's not just pretty. She's ethereal. I shrug, trying to pull my eyes from the trance she's put me in. My hands twitch at the idea of having her coal-black hair wrapped around them.

"Who is?" I know full well who she's talking about, but years of secrecy and hiding emotions have made trusting even those who deserve it difficult for me.

"The pretty girl you're looking at like some sort of snack." Stella shamelessly gestures toward the little mouse. "You know, the one over there with the black hair sipping on an empty glass of ice that you can't seem to take your eyes off. Maybe you should buy the girl a drink."

"No complications," I grunt, then turn to the server beside me and drop a hundred on her tray. "You see that girl there with jet-black hair?"

"Yes, sir."

"Get her whatever she's drinking."

Stella chuckles. "I meant, go up to her."

"No."

"Why not?" Stella pouts.

"I don't exactly put people at ease, Stella. The girl already looks like she's about to bolt."

I've never been a man who makes people comfortable, especially women, and that's how I like it. I revel in causing fear in others, and knowing that no one will ever mess with me again gives me a sense of peace.

But as I stare at the little mouse, her hands shaking while she keeps her eyes fixed on me, something I don't recognize twists in my gut. It's a foreign feeling I haven't experienced in over twenty years.

Axel barks into a laughing fit. "Mik's been hit. Man down."

I should wipe the floor with his sorry ass, so he knows what being hit feels like. Grinding my teeth and clenching my hands, I turn all my venom on him. "Fuck off."

Axel takes a step back, hands raised in the air, a shit-eating grin still plastered on his face. "Relax, buddy. We all gotta go sometime." He drapes his arm around Stella, tugging her to him. "And I'll tell you, being in love is the best fucking thing in the world. Nothing will ever top it."

I grit my teeth and growl. "She's a random chick at a sex club. I'm not in love."

"Everyone's random until they aren't."

"There's a reason Kian is my favorite out of your men, Stella." I ignore Axel and focus on the little mouse again. Good, she got her drink. But it seems like she got something else too.

Standing beside her, taking her attention from me, is a sleazy blond guy. His hand moves to touch her cheek, and she jolts back as if the touch burned her. The guy doesn't seem to get the hint.

My feet move on their own accord. One steel-toed boot hits the hardwood floor in violent step after violent step. The room is still. It doesn't matter that there are over a hundred people in here. All I can focus on is that someone is touching her.

Axel laughs behind me. "Another one bites the dust."

This doesn't mean shit. I'm protecting a woman from the unwanted attention of some dick. I would do this for anyone.

Would you?

A small voice I haven't heard in years taunts me. Fuck. No. No, I fucking wouldn't. Not in a public place, not with witnesses. But the voice telling me this is stupid is overridden by the voice telling me the fucker's brain needs to be bashed until it's a liquid mass pooled by my feet.

The darkness in me bubbles with excitement at the thought of the blood I'm going to spill. It's fucked up how much I enjoy hurting and killing people. The twisted maze in my brain is jumbled unless I can hurt something. Anything.

"Get your hands off her."

The blond guy adjusts the lapels of his suit in some sort of rich preppy boy nonsense. "I'm not sure you know who I am, but you should watch your tone. There are a lot of eligible young ladies here." He turns to the little mouse. "She's already spoken for."

The fucker doesn't get it. I could buy and sell him without blinking. These rich fuckers think wearing expensive clothes and having names attached to some dead motherfucker gives them power. He has shit. Power is when you don't give a fuck. This asshole gives so many fucks that he reeks with it. It's all an image for these trust fund idiots. They want to look dignified when in reality, they're lower than fucking vermin. He's never come across a fucker like me. I'll bash his brains for all his little blue-blood friends to see and not give two shits about what any of them think of me.

My fingers move across the lapel of his suit. Expensive Italian wool, the best of the best. "I don't give a fuck who you are. I'll kill your ass in this room by pulling out your heart and feasting on it, and not one of your rich asshole friends will do anything to stop me."

To emphasize my point, I move my hand down until I grip his wrist. I tilt it back, smiling when his bones snap, and he wails like the little bitch he is. "Just like I predicted. Not one of these fuckers will come to your rescue."

Still holding on to his wrist, I move my hand between his jacket and white dress shirt, remove the wallet from the inside pocket, and pull out his driver's license. "Run off before I have to take things a little further."

"Can I-I have my driver's license?" he stammers.

My hand shakes with the visible tremors of his body. "Nah, this is mine." He's shorter than me, but most people are. At six feet six inches, I always tower over people. I bend down and whisper in his ear. "Make sure you sleep with one eye open."

I place the driver's license in my pocket and smile as he scampers off, nursing his broken wrist.

The alarm buzzes for the prey, and the little mouse rises. She wipes her hands on her pretty dress like she's trying to remove imaginary wrinkles or a stain.

"I'll be seeing you, Little Mouse. Make sure you don't let anyone else touch you because out there, you'll get the animal." I smirk as she swallows, eyes wide, skin turning pink. "I can't wait to see that blush all along your skin as I rip this pretty dress off and fuck you hard against a tree."

She casts her eyes down, focusing on the gold flecks on the marble floor. "Are you taking part in the hunt?"

I touch the delicate skin under her chin with my index finger, raising it so she's forced to look at me. My eyes trail down her body, smiling at the idea of marking her pretty flesh before meeting her dark eyes. "I'll be taking part in hunting you."

Chapter Four

I *love taking part in hunting you."*

The gravel in his voice and the heat in his touch send electric currents surging through my body. The intensity of his eyes has me clenching my thighs and needing a change of panties. He's a big man. He towers over my five feet four-inch height.

When the whistle blows for the prey, I don't bother responding to his comment. I scamper off with the deep sound of his laughter following me. He's got a nice laugh. It's not menacing like his appearance. It's oddly jovial, like a mall Santa's. A guy who can laugh like that can't be all bad, right?

The blond guy's name was Ted. A pompous jerk who wouldn't take my "no, thank you" to his advances. Every time his hot breath landed on my flesh, I wanted to tuck my tail between my legs and run. I've been around men like him before, entitled, arrogant, and convinced they can have whatever they want. I came here to get off, not to get fucked while my vag was dry like the Sahara. Ted is the kind of guy who would stick his dick in a dry vagina and then make his delusional mind believe he's a good lover. He'd probably only last a second too. He gave off one-minute-man energy. But the masked man, he was something else.

Yes, Jason Voorhees energy.

He looks dangerous and not in the "bad boy riding a motorcycle" way, but the "he might chop up bodies and hide them in the cellar" way. Yet even knowing the guy is something strange, I'm drawn to his gritty voice and piercing blue eyes. Those eyes. They can't be normal. Wolves don't even have eyes that blue.

But the devil does.

I line up in formation with twenty or so other women. Our eyes are locked on the prison gladiator-type gate

33

in front of us facing the forest beyond. It's a bit dramatic, but I suppose the club wants to set the mood.

A crackling, static sound comes from the loud-speakers above. "Prey," a deep, ominous voice announces. "It is time to begin." The creaking sound of the metal gates is jarring as they rise, exposing the lush wilderness beyond. "Run far, run fast, run like your life depends on it." A pause for effect. "Because it might."

The tiny hairs on my arms stand at attention, and goose flesh pricks along my skin. My feet make haste over the unleveled slopes and valleys on the ground. There are rock formations ahead of me, pebbled along the lush green grass. Trees complete the landscape, high, looming, and majestic.

Fresh air moves into my lungs as I focus on my breathing. I don't know what I've gotten myself into, but there's a rush, a boost of adrenaline flowing in my veins, a most intoxicating drug I want to be lost in forever.

I haven't been running long, but the concept of running from *something* makes me feel like I've been running for hours. This is a funny game to want to play. I chase to be caught, yet I still run. A sense of danger builds within me. Theoretically, this is a safe situation. The danger is not the running itself but the chase. The anticipation of what will happen once I'm finally caught. This could be a complete bust, a lackluster experience, a waste of time, or it could be what I've been searching for. It all depends on the predator who catches me in his grasp.

There's a sense of freedom running in the wild. It creates a oneness of humanity and nature, a sense of unity. My hands brace against the trees surrounding me so I can propel my legs to run faster and longer.

Growls can be heard off in the distance behind me, forcing me to sprint. I dash through the sanctuary of the trees, stopping at a large elm with lush leaves.

I turn at the sound of rustling leaves behind me. Mikhail and that creepy Ted guy are at my heels. Growls that sound more like wild animals than men escape from the depths of their mouths. Their bodies are poised for a fight. Mikhail isn't wearing a shirt, just dark pants, his feet bare. The sight of him has my body in overdrive as if kerosene has been poured on it before the flame sets it ablaze. A foreign sense of desire and longing lingers beneath the surface.

Mikhail and Ted face off against each other, a rumble in the jungle, two animals poised to attack to see who will be the victor of the spoils of war. Me.

Feminism leaves my body in one fell swoop as I watch in fascination. I should harbor disdain for what these two men are doing, treating me as an object, fighting for rights to me instead of allowing me a choice. But I made a choice by coming here and agreeing to participate in the debauchery.

Ted takes a step forward, and Mikhail doesn't move. He's not wearing the white plastic mask anymore. He's traded it for a ski mask, so I can see the slight curl of his lip, a challenge to Ted. Almost like he's saying, "make my day."

Ted takes another step toward him. His right arm moves to connect with Mikhail's face, but it's stopped mid-air by a large hand wrapped around it.

"Looks like one broken wrist wasn't enough for you," Mikhail snarls. "Let's make it two, shall we?"

A loud snap, this one much more violent than the snap inside the building. A thud as Ted's body crashes to the ground. I watch in fascination and horror as Mikhail's massive hands lift a large branch and bring it down over Ted's head with such force that I'm sure I hear Ted's skull fracture.

The branch falls from Mikhail's hand, the bark now covered in crimson as he bends, pulling Ted by his blood-splattered T-shirt collar. "I don't give a fuck who you are, what your family name is, or how much influence you have. I told your ass to stay the fuck away from her, and you didn't listen."

Mikhail lifts his large fist in the air, and it collides with Ted's face over and over and over until his body goes limp and the eyes burning with fire not too long ago go dark.

Mikhail is a killer. A real-life killer. I should be horrified. I should be disgusted. But I'm wet and excited. My therapist is wrong. This desire isn't normal. I'm fucked in the head. I can't do this. I can't be a party to this. I just watched him beat a man in cold blood.

My gaze moves from the lifeless body on the ground to the piercing ice blue of Mikhail's eyes. "I think you killed him."

The haunting sapphire of his eyes pierces the depths of my soul. "I know."

His voice is calm, cold, and calculated. There is no rage in his words, only fact. He has no remorse, no inclination that what he did was wrong.

He cocks his head. "If it makes it better, he wasn't a good man."

He steps toward me, my back against the tree. The tremors of my hands and the non-stop shaking of my legs tell me I have nowhere to run. But I refuse to give in without a fight. My original instincts were correct about the masked man, yet my body tingles with need and desire, throwing my whole existence on its axis.

I turn to face the large tree before me. My hands are desperate as they crawl at the rough bark, and I pull my body to climb the large trunk.

A firm grip on my ankle pulls me down. "Not so fast, Little Mouse."

Chapter Five

Mikhail

Her ankle is an anchor, keeping her tethered to me. I've got some cleaning up to do after this. I was going to kill Teddy boy, but not this way. The Millers will clean it up. They can't afford to have anyone questioning anything on their property, especially when I've got so much on them. It will cost me some money, but it was worth it. The fucker was told to stay away. He should've listened.

The little mouse nibbles on her bottom lip, tugging it between her bright white teeth.

I want to be the one biting into her flesh. "Looks like the cat caught your tongue, Little Mouse."

Her eyes flash between me and the darkness around us. Growls and screams permeate the air, but all I can focus on is my pretty prey. Her chest rises and falls rapidly, her plump lips open to say something and then quickly close as if unsure her words will do more harm than good.

"Speak."

"Are you going to kill me?"

My lip twitches and turns up in a grin. This is the third time she's put a smile on my face. "I wasn't planning on it. Not really into that snuff shit."

She sighs in relief, the tension in her shoulders evaporating as her guard slips.

"You took my word easily enough. How do you know I'm not lying?"

Her slender shoulders lift as she shrugs. "Don't know. I just do."

I take a step toward her, methodical, precise, and torturously slow so I don't spook her with the words I'm about to utter. "But I *will* hurt you."

Her eyes widen, and she runs.

Howling in the wild, I'm quick on her heels, tackling her to the ground as she reaches the next tree. Her nails dig into the earth to level her. I'm not sure if she wants to be caught or not. She has a safe word, and I'll respect it if it's used, but until then, my beast wants to push her beauty until she breaks. I long to have her beneath me, at my mercy, my pretty little toy.

With one hand, I tear into her dress, shredding it in the middle and exposing her soft white bra and cotton panties to my ravenous gaze. "You came to play, sweetheart. Let the games begin."

My fingers brush against the outside of her panties, and she moans. A sweet sound I long to hear again. But what I want most is to hear it mixed with screams.

I bring my nose to her flesh and inhale the scent of her skin, trailing my tongue along her torso. "Wonder if that pretty cunt of yours will taste as sweet."

She shivers beneath me, but her fight from moments ago has evaporated. I straddle her, my aching cock pressing down on her center. I wrap my hand tightly around her pretty neck, and her eyes widen as I press down. She thrashes against me, her nails digging into my hand, pushing under my skin, and drawing blood in their wake.

"Little Mouse, I like it when you fight."

Her soft gasps for breath drown out the howls in the night and fuel me further. "So pretty. Notice how your fragile gasps for breath make me hard. Your suffering is my pleasure, Mouse." I pull her panties to the side and touch her glistening pussy. "Looks like it makes your cunt wet too."

Her hooded eyes and parted lips send tremors down my spine. The pretty mouse likes this. One finger glides into her soaked pussy and her legs spread open for me, a sweet invitation I won't ignore.

My lips form a smile, and I abandon her pussy, rising and moving her with me. Her eyes round as my hold on her throat tightens, and I drag her up off the ground. I tear the remains of her dress from her body, and she winces as I slam her against the tree. I'm sure the force of my touch mixed with the rough bark of the tree pressed behind her back is painful. There's nothing gentle about my touch, nothing kind or loving, not because I'm a monster but because I don't care to be soft with her. I want to see bruises on her flesh, blood dripping off her skin, the dirt caked on her body.

Her legs move and she kicks me, forcing me to move back. Her nails dig into my biceps, causing blood to trickle down my arm. I release her throat, and she runs again.

"Little Mouse, the more you run, the more I'll make you hurt."

I ignore the rocks and uneven gravel under my bare feet as I chase after her. She's a foot shorter than me, but she's fast. She dashes through the trees, maneuvering the terrain like a damn special ops officer. She looks at me over her shoulder, loses her footing, and falls. As she uses her open palms to lever herself up, I pounce on her like a lion moving on his prey, trapping her body beneath mine. Her ragged breaths permeate my mind and urge the beast within me.

"You can't outrun me, Little Mouse."

A sharp wail pierces the night as her hands dig into my face. "Get off me."

Usually, those words would be enough to make me move as if she'd set me on fire, but this is a hunt, and she hasn't said red. This is part of the game. The depravity that people like us crave. What we need.

Her thumbs press firmly against my eyes. Using my body to trap her under me, I peel her fingers off my face and pin her arms against her body. Growling, I bring my mouth to the top of her tits and bite. The metallic taste of blood floods my mouth, but I refuse to pull away. Her screams echo in the night, and my hard cock throbs with the need to be buried in her pussy.

Abandoning one arm, I push my fingers deep into her cunt, one finger then another, as I trail my nose along her neck and inhale her scent. She withers underneath me, fighting to get free.

One tattoo-covered hand grips her throat again, creating a perfect necklace. "If you want to play games, little girl, you won't like the punishment. I like bad little sluts. More fun to punish." I remove my fingers from her cunt and use the blood trickling on her tit to trail the red crimson onto her face with my fingertips. "You'd look so beautiful drenched in blood."

Her lips part as she inhales a breath. My hands move down her body, trailing the blood. Returning to her warm pussy, I glide one finger inside before adding a second. Her arms rise and she grabs the back of my head. She pulls at the strands of hair as she raises her torso, her dark eyes meeting mine in a challenge. My heart twists at the defiance in her gaze. The girl is a fighter. The girl is on fire. And at this moment, the girl is mine.

She doesn't say anything, just moves her lips closer, bringing them to my throat. Her sharp teeth scrape along my skin, and she bites. The pang of her teeth is sharp, desperate, and needy. She isn't gentle and tears through my flesh like an animal desperate for safety.

A growl escapes me. She isn't fazed by my strong fingers controlling her only source of air. The fact that I could crush her with little to no effort isn't running in the forefront of her mind.

Something foreign registers in my chest, a sharp tug I haven't felt for a very long time. An emotion I steer clear of because it's the cause of destruction, yet I cannot name it. Possession maybe? Ownership perhaps?

I push the notion out of my mind, bring my mouth to the hollow of her neck, and savagely tear into her flesh. Wild, animalistic tendencies overtake me. I'm no longer a man, but a beast unleashed. A monster who'll do whatever he wants without regard or care.

Chapter Six

Fuck. It hurts.

This bite isn't like the one he left on my breast. That was laced with pleasure, but this one is frothing with pain. He's trying to subdue me, to show me he's in charge. That the power lies with him and I'm at his mercy.

His flesh surrounds my nails as I dig further, leaving human claw marks permeating his skin. Leaving vicious tears in his flesh.

"That's it, Little Mouse. Make me bleed."

His fingers work deep in my pussy, his large fingers stretching me. I moan into his skin, yet I refuse to release his flesh. He adds a third finger, filling me. "Look how wet you are for me. All this sweet cum."

He shoves me off him, and my teeth scrape his flesh. I know that must have hurt. His shoulder looks vicious from the souvenir of my teeth. He groans at the pain before forcing me, not so gently, onto the ground. Large hands clasp my abdomen like a vise, holding me in place as he brings his face to my center. His nose trails along my pussy, and the night air permeates with his deep inhale of breath.

The tremors in my body are all-consuming. I'm unsure if they're induced by fear, excitement, or need. Maybe all three. This man can overpower me so easily, and though that should horrify me, it doesn't.

"You smell so sweet, Mouse. I can't wait to taste this pretty little cunt. Lift your legs for me."

I don't move at his commands. "No."

He tilts his head, his face ominous with the mask hiding his expression. "Are we playing a new game, Mouse?"

I don't know what emotion he's wielding behind the shield. Anger? Or amusement?

. . .

My legs are lifted, my feet framing my head. He doesn't wait for me to answer as his tongue lashes at my center, moving up and down my slit with slow movements. The man's feasting on me as if he's starved, and I'm the only thing that satiates his hunger.

"Oh, God."

His hand is on my throat as soon as I speak. His fingers constrict my voice, making the moans barely audible. "Don't worry, sweetheart. I'll make you see heaven once I drag you straight to hell."

He pushes three fingers in and out of me as the tip of his tongue laps at my clit in circles. My body ignites with fresh fire, consuming me, turning me inside out.

"Grab your feet."

My hands move at his command, a marionette controlled by the puppet master. My brain usually runs on all cylinders, but it completely shuts down, only able to function on his orders. I like the feeling of not being able to think but moving in reaction to the words of the man making me come alive in ways no other has before.

His fingers twist within me, pushing up and focusing on my G-spot as his teeth tug at my clit, pulling at it. He slides one finger out of my pussy and circles the lubrication from my cunt around my anus in torturous circles. I'm exposed, helpless, and enthralled by how empowering it is.

"I won't come." I squeak the words.

"Yes, you will."

"No. I'm broken."

He loosens his hold on my throat but continues the assault of his fingers in my pussy.

I take the opportunity to talk, wanting him to know what I desperately need. "I won't come because I'm not scared."

He doesn't answer me. Instead, he tightens his fingers on my throat. The pressure intensifies, and it's no longer just uncomfortable. It's hard to breathe.

I said the wrong thing.

I made him angry.

On what planet did I think it was smart to anger a man I just saw murder someone? Is an orgasm worth death?

My feet shoot down, but he uses his head to elevate me, and his tongue bites hard on my clit. He might rip it off, mutilate me. He probably wouldn't care that I was dead. He'd fuck my corpse and be okay with it. The most fucked up thing about this situation is that I might die, and all I can think about is how fucking good what he's doing to my pussy feels. Tremors shake through me, my hands crawl at the dirt beneath me, and my hips rise in the air, desperate for his mouth on my pussy.

"That's it, Mouse. Fuck my mouth like a dirty little slut. You want to be used, don't you? To be fucked raw, never knowing if I'll snap your pretty little neck. I'm going to use you like the cheap whore you are. Look at you naked on the dirt, begging to be fucked like a pathetic whore. Is that what you want? To be my fuck toy?"

I'm unable to answer, so I buck my hips against him, circling my pussy, desperate to have more of his mouth on me. He presses on my G-spot and sucks my clit, and my body combusts. Over my head, my eyes focus on the formations of stars in the dark sky, making me believe I'm in heaven.

He's right. I'm a whore. I want him to use me, control me, make me come so hard I can't think straight.

Chapter Seven

Mikhail

The girl makes coming look like a damn art form. I reluctantly loosen my grip on her throat and gaze at her as she gasps for breath. Her slender hands reach for the skin, and her fingertips brush along the harsh bruises my hand has left in its wake.

Her eyes connect with mine, and I'm shocked by what I see behind them. She should be scared. She should be terrified. She should despise me. She should run. But all I see in her soft gaze is hunger mixed with wonder. That strange pang in my chest appears again, twisting and creating something I don't recognize. Is it sympathy? Lust?

"What were you saying about not coming?"

She smiles. A genuine smile. Warm, radiant, and kind. It's been a long time since anyone has shown me kindness. But when I gaze into her pretty face, it's all I see.

"That was"—her hand hesitates as she moves it to my face—"wonderful. Thank you."

I want to tell her she's welcome, wrap her in a blanket, and take her home. Treat her right. Make her feel special. But instead, I wrap her soft hair around my hand and yank her head back. "Don't thank me yet. That was just the appetizer."

Raising off the ground, I release my painfully throbbing cock from my pants and present it to her. Her lips part, and before she can say anything, I shove my dick in her pretty little mouth. She trails her velvet tongue around my shaft, coaxing a moan from my lips.

Her hands move up my legs and stop at my ass. Her long nails grip my skin, and she digs into my flesh, pulling my cock further to the back of her throat.

"Open that throat wide for me, Mouse. Take it all in."

Gagging sounds fill the silence between us as saliva drips from the corners of her mouth. She looks like a perfect little porn star, except she's better than anything on film.

My hands fist her hair and I use it as reigns to guide her up and down my shaft. Her long fingers move on my length, adding to the perfection of her warm mouth.

"Fuck, Mouse. If you keep doing that, I'm going to come right down that pretty little throat."

My words egg her on, and instead of backing off, she works her hand and mouth on my cock while her other hand moves to my balls.

She squeals as I yank her head back. Using her long hair, I pull her around, push her against a tree and cup her pussy. "As much as I love your pretty little mouth, what I really want is to fuck this sexy cunt."

Lifting one leg, I slide my cock to her center and impale her with one deep thrust. "Fuck. You're so tight."

She screams as I pound in her cunt with no mercy. She braces her hands against the tree, but I push her with my body, making the tree a barrier so she can't move, can't run, can't do anything but take my cock.

"You're taking me so well, Mouse. Such a good little whore for me. Tell me, Mouse, does it feel good being fucked like a slut in the forest by a stranger?"

Her breath hitches, and she squeaks a small "Yes."

"What are you, Mouse?"

"Horny."

I chuckle at her smart mouth and yank her head back. Her mouth parts at the assault, and I spit, watching the trail of saliva fall from my mouth to hers. "You can do better than that, slut. I want you to tell me exactly what you are."

"I am a dirty little whore who wants you to fuck me so hard I can't walk for days. I want to feel your cock in my tight pussy, to know how you violated me."

The animal rages inside me, taking hold. Pushing her head down on the bark, I fuck her like she means nothing and represents everything. The two dueling sensations of madness and possessiveness wrap around me. My fingers move along her clit as I fuck her with wild abandon, longing to fill her with my cum.

"I'm going to fill you with my cum, Mouse. Fuck you hard and fast, and fill this pussy with my cum."

"Please," she pants.

"Please, what, Mouse? Use your words."

"Please fuck me hard."

Those words are all I need to hear. I hold her head down, making it hard for her to move without scraping her skin. Her hands brace on the tree as I hold one leg and fuck her like she's only there for my pleasure. This is what she wants, to be used, to be owned, and I'm the man to do it.

But even with the brutality of my thrusts and knowing she'll have brutal marks covering her body, I realize that this one taste won't be enough. A lifetime with my little mouse won't be enough. I want to keep a woman for the first time in my life, and the knowledge has me grunting and releasing my cum deep within her pussy.

"Fuck." My ragged breath takes hold of my heart and lungs, and my head falls on top of hers. Her shampoo smells like lavender and honey, and I want to wrap her scent around me like a warm blanket.

I don't know what kind of magic pussy this girl has, but she's got me thinking of flowers and cuddling.

None of that nonsense is who I am or who I want to be. I close my eyes as I try to savor the moment, knowing I'll never have it again, even though I want to.

Chapter Eight

Bree

I gaze at the bruises covering my body in the mirror of the locker room. I'm not the only one battered and bloody—all the women seem to be. Some more than others, but no one has as many scrapes and cuts along their flesh as me. Apparently, I attracted the craziest man of them all. But this man, though volatile, unleashed something impossible. He makes me feel.

Standing in front of the fogged-up mirror, I see the slashes of nails, teeth marks, and tree bark—reminders of my deviance on my skin. My fingers trail the various marks on my flesh. Relief runs through me when I remember I brought loose jogging pants and an oversized black hoodie. Anything tight touching my skin would hurt like hell. I need to treat these when I get home because some of them are deep and look rough.

I tie up my wet hair in a messy bun and grab my duffle bag, shuffling out of the locker room. Casting my head down, I avoid looking directly at anyone walking by. Making eye contact with anyone who might suspect what I did in the forest makes me uncomfortable. I don't understand why I'm sheepish about what I did—this place is created for it. But shame washes over me at the knowledge of what I like. I fucked a murderer, and my morals went right out the window. Sure, Ted was a criminal—well, I don't know for sure, but the way his sleazy self kept coming on to me, it was pretty evident the guy couldn't take no for an answer. Although, killing him is worse. Or maybe it isn't. I'm not going to feel bad about guys like him getting what they deserve.

"Hey, sweetheart." I look up to see the pretty waitress from earlier and can't help returning her warm, sweet smile. Her eyes work their way along my exposed neck and face. "Looks like you had a little too much fun, huh?" Her hands move to her pocket, and she pulls out a small cylinder-shaped container of cream before handing it to me. "Put this on all your cuts and scrapes. It will help them heal better."

I take the small container and turn it in my hand. "What is it?"

"It's like polysporin, only much stronger."

I smile at her as I place the container in the pocket of my hoodie. "Some weird hunt club magic?"

"You could say that. It's completely safe. I've been using it for a while."

"What?" I'm unable to hide the shock in my voice. "Sorry, I just assumed you worked here. You look—"

"Innocent?"

"Well, yes."

She laughs, the sound melodic. "It's always the innocent ones." She places a hand on my shoulder and brushes by me.

"Hey, what's your name?"

"It's Noelle."

"That's pretty. Nice to meet you, Noelle."

I push through the large doors of the manor and into the crisp night air. The sense of danger and the rush of excitement no longer propels my tired body. All I want is my warm bed and my giant, cuddly comforter.

I reach into my duffle bag and dig out my phone to order an Uber.

"I'll drive you home."

I jump at the deep voice and look up to see Mikhail. He's dressed in a black suit, his white plastic mask on his face—a mirage hiding the animal.

"I'm fine, thank you."

He tugs my duffel from me and slings it onto his shoulder before taking my hand in his. "You seem confused, Mouse. You assumed I was offering. I wasn't. It was more of a command."

The fucking nerve of this man. "I'm not your property. You seem to think you can tell me what to do."

"Little Mouse, it's cute how you're trying to stand up for yourself, but how about we try a little honesty? You like it when I tell you what to do. Bet if I take your sweatpants off right now, your cunt will be soaking for me."

He trails his hand along the elastic of my pants, fingers barely touching my skin. His finger dips into my sweatpants and glides inside my panties. He pulls his hand out and places his wet finger in front of my face. "Like I said. Dripping."

"That doesn't mean you can boss me around."

"Get on your knees."

"Excuse me?"

His hand moves to the back of my head and fists my bun before he pushes me down to the ground.

"You're talking a little too much, so maybe you need to fill your mouth. Take my cock out, slut."

My treacherous body betrays me as my hands move to his zipper. He's not wearing any underwear. My hand fists his enormous dick as I gaze up at him.

"So pretty on your knees for me. Start sucking like the good little cock whore you are."

My mouth opens, and he slams into me, forcing my head back. His cock is huge, and I can barely take him with the full force of his hips fucking my throat as if it's my pussy. Saliva overflows my mouth, and I can't breathe.

His fingers pinch my nostrils, making it even harder to inhale. "Eyes on me, Mouse. I want you to look at me while you choke on my cock. I could kill you this way. What do you think about that? You should see how cute you look, a perfect shade of red."

He's fucking crazy. He pushes more of his cock into my mouth, and I make pathetic noises as he assaults me.

"But you know what? As pretty as the red is on your face, I prefer the color blue."

He may be deranged, but I squeeze my thighs together, desperate for relief.

He laughs as he gazes down at me. "This making you horny? Rub your clit. If you come before you pass out, I'll let you go."

My fingers dive into my pants and move on my clit while he fucks my mouth with no mercy. My body is on fire, and my fingers are accelerant. I'm so fucked up that the idea of dying makes me explode with pure ecstasy.

Mikhail barks out a laugh and lets go of my nostrils. "Good girl."

Why are those words so sexy coming from a man like him? All his filthy talk with these rare moments of praise is enough to make me want to bend over and let him fuck me like he did in the woods.

His warm hands grip my biceps, and he lifts me off my feet. "Show me which finger made you come?"

I lift my hand to him, and he delicately takes it in his, his piercing blue eyes locked with mine as he sucks my finger slowly into his mouth. The sight is pure eroticism.

"Let's go." He pulls me toward a silver Porsche and forces me into the passenger seat. He circles the car, climbs behind the wheel and starts the engine.

Without another word, he steers the Porsche into the night.

The drive to my apartment is quiet. Mikhail doesn't say a word, and I like it that way. I don't know what to say to him anyway. The man is an enigma. When he's taking control and fucking me, he's dangerous, lethal even. But the moments when he makes sure I'm warm in the car and the way he gently touches the scrape from the tree on my face tell me that deep down, there's something softer beneath his deranged appearance.

I unlock the door and turn to shut it on him. "Well, thank you."

He jams his foot to stop the door from closing. "You're not staying here."

"Where do you expect me to go? This is where I live."

"I don't like this neighborhood. It's rough, and there are some dangerous types hanging around here."

I smile smugly. "I know. One of them is trying to get into my apartment as we speak."

"Get what you need, and I'll get the rest later. You're coming home with me."

The fuck I am. Who does this guy think he is? "Just because I fucked you doesn't mean you get to tell me what to do."

His blue eyes blaze as he uses the force of his body to push me back and enters my apartment. His hand disappears behind him, and I hear the lock click into place.

"What do you think you're doing?"

"I won't tell you again, Mouse. Pack your shit, and let's go." He unbuttons his suit jacket, and a shiny gun in a holster is attached to the side of his right hip. "Pack your shit."

Something in my broken brain demands I find out what will happen if I reject Mikhail's demand. "No."

In a blink of an eye, his forearm is against my throat, my back is to the wall, and his gun is pointed directly at my pussy. "What are you doing?"

"You seem to think I don't get what I want. You saw what I did in the woods, didn't you? How easily I killed a man and walked away with no remorse. I'm used to getting what I want, Mouse. So pack your shit." He glides the barrel along my pussy, pressing the tip right onto my clit. "You want to play Russian roulette, Mouse? I could make you cum with this gun. Fuck your pussy with it."

"You're certifiable."

"Yes, Mouse, we've already established I'm crazy. So if you don't want a loaded gun up your wet cunt, pack a fucking bag."

I should say no. I should fight. But God help me, this man has awakened something, and I don't want to let it go.

He cocks the gun, and I jump. "What's it going to be, Mouse?"

Chapter Nine

Mikhail

She probably thinks I'm a fucking rapist and kidnapper. Technically, I didn't rape her. It was coercion, and I would have backed off if she'd said no. There's no way I'd hurt a fucking hair on her head in anger or frustration. She said she needs to be scared to come, and I'm going to give her that.

There's something about being able to be my true fucked up self with her that's beyond liberating. The girl sings to my deranged soul, and there's no way I'm letting her go. Meeting the little mouse is like someone setting me free from the bars holding me captive most of my life.

Maybe I wouldn't be like this had my life not been fucked up. I trained to be a killer before I even kissed a girl. My most impressionable years were drenched in blood, murder, and cruelty.

Growing up without a loving mother or father, my only role model was a ruthless criminal who didn't even love his own flesh and blood. To Sergei Fedorov, those around him were pawns and foot soldiers used to advance his position of power and persuasion. I was fine with living a life without comfort or joy, but then this little mouse, with her sweet face and smart mouth, caught my eye, and now everything is fucked up and confusing.

She hasn't said a thing since we left her apartment. Usually, I don't mind silence. I prefer it, but I don't like that the little mouse won't talk to me. I guess I can't blame her. I did tell the girl I'd put a bullet in her cunt if she didn't come with me. She doesn't know I wouldn't do it. How could she know? All I've done from the moment I saw her is be a psychotic dick. She probably thinks I'm a raging lunatic.

I push the pasta across the island to her. "It's pretty good. I've got a chef who comes by twice a week and stocks the fridge."

She pushes the food on her plate with her fork, her eyes cast down.

"I'm not going to bite you."

Her head shoots up, and she lifts one eyebrow.

I raise my hands and chuckle. "Okay, I'm not going to bite you at this moment. Eat. And drink your water. You need to stay hydrated after what happened today, and you need some food in you. I don't want you to get sick."

"You're concerned with my water consumption after you threatened to kill me with a loaded gun?"

"Correction. I threatened to fuck your pussy with a loaded gun."

She pushes her food aside and stands, moving around the table and stopping between my parted legs. Her hands move through my hair in a gentle manner. She trails her hands down my neck and around the edge of my mask. I allow her to explore, but as her fingers move past the edges to remove my mask, my hands shoot up to grasp hers.

I jump off the stool and away from her. "What the fuck do you think you're doing?"

"I want to see your face."

"No one sees my face."

She bites her bottom lip, gazing at me. The silence is deafening, and as I'm about to break it, she speaks. "If you want me to stay, you need to show me who you are. You pulled a fucking gun on me. You degraded me. You bit me, scared me, and I let you. I'll keep letting you, but I need to know who you are. Unless you're a psycho who wants to play with his next kill before he offs her. Then I guess you don't owe me shit, but if you want more with me, you need to be real. I want to know what you're hiding from the world. I don't want you hiding it from me."

"No one sees my face. My rules."

She moves away from me, walking back to her side of the island and then further away to the front door. "Then I'm not staying here. I don't want anything to do with you."

Bree

I grab the overnight bag Mikhail made me pack and head toward the front door. But then warm hands encircle my wrist, pulling me back. I turn and see those bright wolf eyes glaring back at me.

"You're not going anywhere. I'm not done with you yet."

"I don't give a fuck what you're done with because I'm done with you."

An animalistic growl fills the ten-million-dollar penthouse apartment. Whatever Mikhail does, he's good at it based on how posh this place is. He lifts me off the ground and throws me over his shoulder.

"Put me down."

"You don't want me to put you down, Mouse. You want me to blow your mind with another orgasm."

"I do not," I lie.

As much as Mikhail infuriates me, he's also the only man who's ever made me come. Not only did he make me come, he made me come three times in less than twenty-four hours. I don't want to be pathetic, but when a guy fucks like that, you don't want to say no.

His hands move up the back of my leg to my ass, and before I know it, my jogging pants and panties are pulled down to my ankles, with me still over his shoulder.

"What do you think you're doing?"

"I'm going to make you come all over my tongue. You got any objections, Mouse? Or will you be a good girl and let Daddy taste his favorite dessert?"

The balcony door opens, and the fresh air hits me like a wave. "You can't fuck inside like a normal person?"

"This isn't for my pleasure, darling. It's for yours."

A vicious scream leaves my lips as my body is dangled off the balcony railing. I hang there with only my ankle held by Mikhail. He doesn't say anything but moves his tongue on my pussy like an artist. I don't know how the man knows how to eat pussy like this, but it's something else. My entire body shakes with need and fear as I stare down at the people walking on the sidewalk beneath me. They look like insignificant ants.

Looking down seventy-two floors while dangling from the balcony of a Highrise in Millennium Park is traumatizing to an average person. But I'm not average. I'm screaming in ecstasy while the devil makes me come for the fourth time.

"Wouldn't it be nice to experience an orgasm while you plummet to your death, Bree? Imagine the liberation."

"You're fucking crazy."

A long swipe of my pussy with his eager, talented tongue. "Am I, Bree? Do you think I'm the crazy one for doing what you want? You need the fear, Bree. You need the danger. That's how I know no matter what you say about leaving me, you never will because I'm the only man who can give you what you want. Most men won't do the things you need. They have morals or a sense of guilt. That's what's great about me, Bree. I don't have either. All I have is a hedonistic desire to make you come until you can't think straight."

He lifts me and places me gently back on my feet. I face him, exposed from the waist down, my legs weak from the most mind-blowing sexual act of my life.

He shoves his finger into my pussy, pushing me to the glass sliding balcony door. "I'm gonna take you to bed and care for the wounds on your body. You're going to be a good girl and get a good night's sleep, and the first thing I'm doing in the morning is fucking this pussy of mine until you learn to do as you're told."

Mikhail walks me to the bathroom and removes a towel from the rack. He spreads it on the counter before lifting and placing me on it. A drawer opens, and he takes out a jar like the one Noelle gave me at The Hunt Club. "Take off your hoodie."

I slide the sweater up my body and over my head, sitting completely naked and exposed to him. His touch is gentle and soothing as he places the cream on my scrapes and rubs it in.

I thought it would sting, but it doesn't. It's cool and refreshing. "What is this stuff?'

"It's a stronger version of polysporin. They give this shit to medics in battle. It has a little extra kick to it. I'll put some on again tomorrow. Turn around for me." I jump off the counter and turn. Mikhail hisses as he brushes his fingers on various parts of my back. "I'm sorry. I didn't think I was that rough. Things get out of hand with the hunt, and when you told me about the fear thing, it released something in me."

I shrug. "No biggie. I knew what I was getting into."

"Maybe, but I don't do this to women, Bree. This isn't who I am."

I frown. "How do you know my name?"

"I have my ways. I usually have no problem finding out things about people. Like I know you live alone, had a dog named Buster but he died a year ago, and you haven't been able to get a new one because you work so much. You're a nurse. Pediatrics. You love kids, and you bake a mean chocolate chip cookie."

"Do you work for the CIA?"

Mikhail laughs. "More like I'm probably watched by the CIA." He puts the cap back on the cream and kisses my right shoulder. "All done. It's late, and you need your rest. We can talk more in the morning."

* * *

"It's so dark. Why does Mommy sound like that? She said to stay here. I've got to stay here. They can't get me here."

The sound of a deep voice in terror wakes me in the middle of the night. I turn over, and Mikhail, now wearing a white ski mask, is muttering, his body covered in a sheen of sweat.

I place my hand on his shoulder. "Mikhail."

Suddenly, my back is pressed against the mattress. Mikhail's large frame looms over me, his body pressing down on mine as his fingers grip my throat with such force they take my breath away. It's almost like he isn't here anymore, completely gone. He's not even the monster I saw in the woods. He's something else, something darker, more dangerous, and utterly insane. He lines his cock to my entrance and pushes into me.

"Mikhail," I croak, desperately trying to get him to snap out of it.

He isn't there. All I see is his face covered with the mask and piercing blue eyes burning into my brain. His haunting wolf eyes are the last thing I see, and the darkness takes over.

Chapter Ten

Mikhail

Dread rushes through me like a tornado. My heart stops. Panic surges in frantic waves as I place my fingers on her bruised neck to check her pulse. My fingers gently rub at the angry marks left behind in their wake. A sharp inhale of relief as I realize she's still breathing. The idea of hurting her is repugnant to me, the vilest thing I could imagine, all my nightmares coming to fruition.

Her angelic face looks so peaceful. My hard cock still impales her tight cunt. I should dismount and let her sleep in peace, but my need for her is all-consuming.

All I can focus on is her body, her tight cunt, her puckered nipples, and the pretty bruises covering her creamy skin.

I fuck her slowly, wanting to savor her in every way. I know what I'm doing is wrong, demonic even. She's asleep due to my hands suffocating her, but I don't care. I still want to come inside her, fill her up. Her hard nipples tempt my fingers as they slowly roam up her stomach. I take the soft flesh in my hand. I pinch her pink nipples between my fingers and groan at how sexy she looks. My marks cover her skin, my passion a road map along her flesh.

The thrusts of my hips speed up, and I fuck her mercilessly. She'll be sore tomorrow from how my cock drills into her sweet pussy with no remorse or mercy.

This girl has wrapped herself around my soul, and I know she won't accept me for long. I'm a novelty she'll tire of. How could a beauty like this crave a monster like me? It simply isn't something long-lasting.

My balls tighten with the tight grip of her sexy cunt, and my lips descend on her skin. I place chaste kisses along her soft flesh until I meet her rose-colored lips with mine and come deep in her pussy.

I should stop here, but I can't. I want more of her. I need to see more of her. My lips move down her body, exploring every inch of her with my mouth until I'm in front of her sweet cunt. My cum leaks out of her, proof that I fucked her while she was passed out. As sexy as it is to watch my cum drop out of her cunt, I want her to have it. A sick compulsion to make sure she knew I was here in the morning. To feel my cum dripping from her pussy when she's wide awake.

I push my cum back into her pussy and clean it off my finger, tasting the two of us together. Fucking delicious.

I kiss her on her lips before pulling her to me and falling sound asleep for the first time in a very long time.

The sun blares into the room, and I move to squeeze Bree to me, but my arms are empty. My eyes shoot open, and instead of seeing her sexy body in my bed, there's a piece of paper with two sentences.

Mikhail,

Thanks for the good time, but I'm not into secrets. If you're ready to tell me what I want to know, come find me.

Bree.

Chapter Eleven

W hoa, what happened to you?" Claire, one of the nurses on duty, asks. Her eyes roam my body, and her gaze is curious and worried.

"I went a little too hard at the gym."

She eyes me suspiciously. I'm confident she knows I'm lying. Bruises make sense from the gym, but bite marks do not. "If you need me to look at them, let me know."

"I already took care of them but thank you."

I'm grateful when she nods and drops the conversation. Her eyes move down the corridor. "Check out that guy. Someone should tell him it's a little too early for a Halloween costume.

My eyes dart up from the computer, and I freeze as I stare at Mikhail heading directly toward me. "It's okay. I know him. He's a little corky."

Who does he think he is bringing his shit to my place of work? Not everyone is a rich spoiled asshole. Some of us need our jobs.

I storm up to him, my nails digging into the flesh around his elbow as I pull him into a room and close the door behind us.

Great. I didn't notice it was a storage closet. I lock the door so we can't be interrupted and turn my gaze on him. "What the fuck are you doing here?"

His wolf eyes flash with anger. Those eyes aren't normal. That blue is alien. "I woke up, and you were gone."

I shrug, keeping my distance from him. "I had to work."

He takes a step toward me, forcing me to take one back to avoid his all-consuming presence. "That's not what your note said."

"I'm fully aware of what the note said. Now leave."

He bares his teeth, transforming from man to beast right in front of me. He takes another step forward. "You're never leaving me."

My voice shakes as I talk, not because I'm scared but because being in his presence makes my body a pathetic, whimpering puddle of mush. "Listen, it was fun, but I'm not your property. I'm done, and you need to leave."

He doesn't say anything. He moves closer still, one step, two steps until my back is to the wall and his body surrounds me. He has me trapped again, caught up with need for him.

"What are you gonna do? Rape me, Mikhail?" I regret the words as soon as they leave my mouth.

"I'm not a rapist."

"Then leave me the hell alone."

Whatever remorse he might have felt a moment ago is gone. He turns those ice-blue eyes on me, and a grunt leaves his lips. The hard length of his body presses against mine, and his scent is intoxicating—lemons, peppermint, and Mikhail. I must ask him what soap he uses because it's incredibly unique.

I start to speak, but I'm paralyzed when the light reflects off the blade of a sharp, silver hunting knife.

"Fuck you, Bree. I'm a lot of things, but a rapist isn't fucking one of them. You don't know the shit I've gone through in my life. You think it's easy seeing the shit I've seen and done and casually talking about it with someone over a cup of coffee? As if murder for hire is the same job as being a mailman?"

Mikhail's free hand moves down my body, pushing the hem of my skirt above my waist before he switches hands with the knife. His forearm presses against my throat, and—oh, God—he moves the sharp tip of the blade softly along my pussy. "You want to know what rape is like, Bree?"

Jesus Christ, I'm wet. I have a man whose face I've never seen holding a knife against my pussy, and instead of being scared, I want to know what he'll do next because I'm turned the fuck on.

Mikhail barks a laugh as if he can read every thought running wild in my mind. "You like this, don't you, Mouse?"

"Yes."

"Well, since you think I'm a rapist, I'm going to need you to beg for it. Beg me to fuck you like the good little whore you are."

"I'm not fucking a man who won't show me his face."

He presses the knife to my pussy, the blade gliding along my panties. The tear from the knife on the fabric fills the room. Oh, God, he just ripped my panties off with a knife, and all I can think about is his cock buried in me.

He moves the blade gently along my pussy, careful not to hurt me, just a soft caress. "So let me get this straight. The deal breaker isn't that I kill people for a living but that I won't show you my damn face?'

A moan escapes my lips, "Yes. What if you're ugly? A girl has to know what she's investing in."

"You don't care about looks, Bree. If you did, you would've fucked Ted in the woods." Mikhail turns his face up to the ceiling as if contemplating something. "I still would have killed him because he touched you, and I don't like people touching what's mine. But don't worry, Bree. I'm not ugly. My face isn't riddled with scars. My wounds are on the inside. It's not my face that's repugnant. It's my heart. Now, why don't you be a good girl and beg Daddy to fuck your pretty cunt until you forget all this nonsense and scream my name."

I want to fight him, tell him this is not happening, but God help me, I can't. "Please."

"Going to have to do better than that, Mouse. Beg like the good slut I know you are."

"Please fuck me. I don't care what you use or how you do it. Just fuck me. I'll be a good little slut for you, Daddy. I'll gag on your thick cock. I'll let you mark me. I'll even fuck your gun. Just please fuck me the way only you know how."

I moan as he fills me with his cock and moves his blade to my throat. "I like you like this, Bree. My good little whore. Look how well we fit together. You know you're mine. You were mine with that first look. As much as you want to run from me, you won't because no one will ever give you what you need. You crave my cock like a pathetic whore, don't you, Bree?"

"Yes," I pant.

The sting of the blade pricks my collarbone. "I like hurting you, Mouse. Don't know what's wrong with me, but when you bleed for me, my cock gets hard. I like the fear in your eyes right before you come for me. You're the perfect slut, Bree. My perfect little whore. You want me, Bree. There's no one you'll ever want more than me. And if you ever did, I'd slit their throats with the knife I just used on your flesh."

My nails dig into his neck, pressing down, wanting him to feel the need for pleasure mixed with pain that we share. He fucks me against the wall while he moves his hand holding the blade to my clit. My body and mind are in unison—this is the man I want, the man I need. My heart constricts at the pain he must endure to hide himself from me, to be ashamed of who he is. I want to know him, all of him, not just the fractured moments of unadulterated pleasure he provides me.

He rubs the handle of the knife against my clit. My body is transcending, my mind reaching new peaks, and the pleasure surging through me is undeniable and forceful.

"Come for me, Bree. Come for me like the good little slut you are."

I clamp down on his neck and bite to muffle my scream as I come on his dick.

"That's it, baby. Come for Daddy. Show me how much you love my cock in your cunt. How you crave it. I'm going to fill my pussy now, baby."

Mikhail's words are feral as he releases into me. He pulls out and falls to his knees. His hot mouth latches on to my cunt, sending new sensations up my spine.

"Let it drip into my mouth, Bree. I want all that cum. Push it out for me, baby."

I watch in fascination as cum leaks from my pussy directly into his open and waiting mouth. "Oh, God. I think this is the hottest thing I've ever seen."

Once Mikhail has his fill, he rises and stares at me. He fists my hair, yanking it back to tilt my head, and my mouth opens for him as he pinches my nostrils. Standing here with my mouth open wide, I watch with pure unbridled passion as the cum from his mouth falls into mine before he kisses me hard. The kiss is consuming, passionate, and filthy. It represents the depravity of who we are, who we will always be.

"You're my good girl, aren't you, Bree?'

I nod, knowing that no matter what I say or do, every part of me belongs to this man.

"I never want to hear you talk about not being mine again, Bree, because I'll never let you go." He pushes away from me and tucks his cock back into his pants.

The door lock clicks, letting me know our time is up. Mikhail holds onto the door before turning to me and shocks me by removing his mask.

The man is a work of art. A chiseled jaw, high cheekbones, five o'clock shadow on his jaw. His face would make the most handsome man in Hollywood weep.

I walk to him, my hands tentative as I cup his stubbled cheeks. Gazing firmly into his blue irises, I tell him something I'm not sure he's heard before. "You're beautiful."

"Beauty is skin deep, Bree. Don't let the charade fool you. I'm a monster."

"Maybe, but you're my monster. I want to know you, Mikhail. I don't want you to hide from me. You don't have to."

"I'll pick you up after work."

And with that, I'm alone in the dark storage closet with a full heart and a satiated pussy.

Chapter Twelve

Mikhail

Bree places her finished plate in the dishwasher before turning and circling her arms around my waist. A hug. She's hugging me. It's odd for a man in his thirties to be confused by such a simple gesture. But simple touches filled with care are foreign to me.

"...was lovely. Thank you."

I tug her toward me. I feel like I've all the riches in the world because she's in my arms. "The company is even better."

She tilts her head and gazes at me, her eyes full of compassion and warmth. "It's time to spill the beans."

I appreciate her light nature in approaching a serious subject, but I understand that what I'm about to tell her may change how she sees me forever.

I kiss the top of her head and take her hand, walking her to the couch. "This is hard for me. My best friends haven't even heard the entire story. I'm not sure I ever want to tell them."

"Whatever you tell me, Mikhail, it stays between us."

"And I want the woman I love to really see me."

She clasps her heart. "You love me?"

"I'm not sure I fully comprehend what love is, but I'm assuming that's what this is. You're my breath, Bree. The idea of being without you is enough to stop my black and broken heart. You're the moon in my perpetual darkness, the beacon of light that gives me hope."

I shift on the couch, pulling her onto my lap. "Do you know what a death rattle is? It's the last sound someone makes before dying. A futile attempt to swallow, cough, or clear saliva from one's throat. I have been running to and from the sound my entire life, living as a ghost so the sound could never touch me.

Now I'd welcome that same nightmare with open arms as long as you're safe from it. I was dead before you, Bree. You gave me life, and I'll fucking burn the earth before I'd let anything ever happen to you. I love you, Bree, because that's the only word that makes sense now, my heart only beats for you. I love you so fucking much, I can't see straight."

Bree

My heart soars. They didn't make that up. Hearing those words from Mikhail is like winning the jackpot in the biggest lotto the world has ever known.

I brush my hand along his cheek. The man is beautiful without the damn mask. Not that I mind the mask. It's hot, and I'll be asking him to wear it sometimes. But sitting here, staring at his face—a face he only shows me—does something to me I didn't think was possible. "I love you, too."

"You might not love me once you hear the whole story."

"I'll love you," I reassure him.

"My father killed my father when I was ten."

My hand flies to my mouth to conceal the gasp trying to escape my lips.

"I had no idea he was my father at the time. My step-father, I guess, raised me. He was a good man. Maybe under him, I could have been something better. We were living in America at the time. We'd fled Russia. It was hard starting over. People rarely understand how hard it is for immigrants and their children. Children usually adapt, but the parents suffer. There's always this sense of not belonging, no matter what you do. A notion that you're never home, just a permanent tourist. It's even harder when you don't have money. We were poor. We always had the basics—food, clothes, and shelter—but there was no money for anything else. But I had a lot of love. My parents were kind, honest people who truly cared for me." He waves his hand around the room. "I'd give up all this just to see my mother's smile again."

I place my head on his chest, sensing it will probably be easier on him to speak if he isn't forced to stare at me.

"We were setting up for a movie night, a small indul-gence my parents allowed us to have. Nothing grand by any means, but it was something I always looked forward to. That was when my mother rushed me into a closet to hide me, and they killed both my parents, brutally, without mercy, and took me. I was taken back to Russia. Back to a man who murdered my mother because she took something that belonged to him. He didn't want me because I held value for him. He wanted me because it boosted his ego. So, for the next twenty-ish years, I worked for a man who was my biological father but treated me as a trained mercenary. A cold, heartless killer who murdered on his demand."

Hearts must break because I feel mine shatter into a million pieces for Mikhail. I cry for the little boy he was and the horrors he's had to endure. My heart breaks that he's sharing something so traumatic with me because he cares about me. He's enduring pain because he wants me to have what I want—to understand him, the real him, all of him.

"I have two brothers who think I'm their best friend."

"What? Have you met them?'

"Yes. They're my two best friends."

I push off him, my hands on his firm chest. "Wait, you've gone all these years without telling your family that they're your family."

"Blood doesn't make family. They have my back, and I've got theirs."

"You don't want to tell them the truth?"

Mikhail grabs my legs, moving one on each side of his thighs. "No. I don't. They are my brothers in every way that matters. There's no point bringing up the past. Besides, Sergei was someone I never wanted to claim as a father." His hands brush my hair off my shoulders, and he kisses the side of my neck. "I think I'm done talking. I think it's time I vent my frustrations on your perfect little cunt."

I wrap my hands around his neck and giggle. "I love you."

"I love you too, Little Mouse."

Epilogue

B ree

U sually, Mikhail picks me up from work, but he texted earlier and told me he had some business come up and couldn't make it. So, I grabbed some Chinese food, and now I'm going to sit at home in front of the television and watch some sappy chick flick.

I walk into the apartment and turn the lock when a hand covers my mouth and drags me backward. The intruder moves back when I kick him in the shin, and I dive into the bedroom where Mikhail installed a safe

95

room. But right before I get to the door, the guy pulls me by my leg and shoves a gun in my face.

"Open your mouth, or I'll blow your head off." His voice is barely audible.

"My husband will cut tiny pieces off you and make you eat it before it puts you six feet under."

"I'll be long gone before that'll ever happen."

Tears I'm desperate to keep in check glide down my cheeks as the barrel of the gun is forced into my mouth. His hands move down my legs and he pushes my skirt up before he tears my panties off with one hand.

This guy is going to rape me. Dread consumes my body and shame fills me because even though I'm terrified, my body still responds to the horrific act. Since being with Mikhail, I've become comfortable with my sexual needs and desires. We talked about my rape fantasies and playing out a scene. Those situations are my choice, but this—this isn't what I want.

I'm mortified at my arousal as his fingers move through my folds.

"Such a good girl." He moves off me, his hand moving to the zipper of his pants. "Move, and I'll shoot."

I'm frozen, unable to move as he shoves his cock in my pussy and moves the gun in and out of my mouth. "Don't make me do anything rash. I don't want to kill you accidentally. A stupid move could make me pull the trigger, and we wouldn't want your brains on the pretty marble floor."

I try to stay immobile, but the fear mixed with his cock...wait, a minute. I reach up, pulling at the black ski mask covering his face, and sigh in relief.

Without saying a word, he removes the gun from my mouth, and presses his lips to mine. The kiss is full of passion, desperation, and need. But most of all, it's full of love. The ocean's worth of love we have for each other.

"Surprise! How did you know it was me?"

"Your cock. You think I wouldn't know my husband's dick?"

"You're so fucking wet. Just like I knew you would be."

"You're crazy, you know that?"

"Yes," Mikhail says, kissing the tip of my nose. "And you love it."

"I do."

The Dangerous Sinner Series

These are all stand alones within the same wold.

Made in United States
North Haven, CT
14 August 2023

40302973R00063